Mimi: The Mouse at Sacred Heart

Story by the
Lower School Students of
Convent of the Sacred Heart

Illustrated by
Karin Randlett

Published by Convent of the Sacred Heart
1 East 91st Street
New York, NY 10128

Conceptualized, compiled, edited and produced
by the book committee:
Jane Bischoff
Laurie Norman
Rosemarie Zanghellini

Design by The Blank Page, New York, NY
The body copy for this book is set in 13 point ITC Officina Serif

Mimi: *The Mouse at Sacred Heart* is a book written by the children of Sacred Heart for the children of Sacred Heart. The story is based on love and friendship. The genesis of this book started with the 125th Sacred Heart Anniversary Committee meeting in late October 2006. What could be done by the Lower School students as a class project in honor of this special celebration? Rosemarie Zanghellini, a parent, conceived the wonderful idea of a book that would not only be a testament to the community spirit of Sacred Heart, but, more importantly, would inspire the Lower School students to love books and writing by being part of the creative process and seeing the tangible result of their efforts.

In early November, with the hard work and determination of Rosemarie, a book committee was formed that included Jane Bischoff, Laurie Norman, and Rosemarie. An outline for the story was drafted, and the Lower School homeroom teachers generously agreed to work with their students on the contribution of their classes. Each class from grades one to four wrote a chapter that had an assigned story outline and location in the school. The three kindergarten classes wrote poetry on a given theme. And, finally, the two pre-kindergarten classes helped to choose names for characters. Every Lower School student was able to contribute.

The students' inspired stories came together as this book with the tireless editing of Laurie Norman and Rosemarie Zanghellini. While not everything is exactly as it was originally written by the students, the words and ideas of the student are at the heart of this book. In the same spirit, our artist, Karin Randlett, started in January to work on her wonderful illustrations. She completed the artwork in record time. Thanks to the dedication of each person on this project, we were able to finish a two-year project in five months.

Thanks go to Patricia Hult and Monica Padmanabha and the Sacred Heart faculty and staff, along with the advancement office, who gave us support and encouragement from the start of this project. Special thanks to Kira Egan, Christi Gowen, and, especially, Laurie Norman, Lower School librarian, who gave so generously of her time and talented editing skills, and whose rich knowledge of Sacred Heart proved so helpful. Additional thanks to Victoria Wells, who so kindly followed through with suggestions as the book moved along, as well as to the many parents and friends of Sacred Heart without whose wonderful spirit this book could not have been completed.

The final acknowledgement, of course, must go to the inspiration of this book-the Lower School students of Convent of the Sacred Heart.

This book is dedicated

with much love to

Pat Hult

for her 30 years of commitment

and devotion to the girls

of Sacred Heart.

On behalf of the countless families

whose lives have been touched

by her guidance and affection,

we say, "Très bien."

Many thanks to the Lower School teachers who helped make this book a reality

Ms. Jennifer Barrese
Mrs. Lovella Beres
Ms. Dominique Cortese
Ms. Kira Egan
Ms. Janet Egyhazi
Mrs. Alison Henry
Ms. Amy Herman
Mrs. Regina Holohan
Ms. Eliza Hurd
Ms. Kristen Jessop
Ms. Anne King
Ms. Jennifer Kohler
Mrs. Amy Lederman
Mrs. Sarah Lubeley
Ms. Lauren Mara
Ms. Anne McDonough
Mrs. Laurie Norman
Mrs. Colleen O'Sullivan
Ms. Amy Pacula
Ms. Chloe Pashman
Mr. Richard Rodney
Ms. Catherine Rowland
Mrs. Kathy Saffian
Mrs. Linda Santoro
Mrs. Francesca Westenberg
Mrs. Carol Wheeler

Pre-Kindergarten 3's *Class of 2021*	Josephine Buccini Caroline Burke Charlotte Croft Alejandra de la Fuente Sloan Duvall	Samantha Gilfond Federica Hernandez Preston Manna Sasha O'Halloran Carolina Pachetti	Evelyn Robert Pilar Rossi Isabella Rubin
Pre-Kindergarten 4's *Class of 2020*	Leilani Blakeman Cecilia Bohan Anne Mairead Burwell Sarah Carter Catherine Coyne Hadley Guthrie	Nathalie Hartman Margot Healy Rebecca Lytle Phoebe Martin Natalie McCormick Kalila Meguid	Kristin O'Donoghue Hope Petralia Margaret Robertshaw Elena-Grace Rossi Elizabeth Weise
Kindergarten *Class of 2019*	Sydney Acevedo Catherine Anderson Elena Maria Baldwin Nayla Boorady Virginia Breen Hyland Brown Alexandra Brumbaugh Fiona Calcagnini Sophie Cestari Kate Clark Georgia Coleman Isabella Cruz Paige Duffy Isabelle Edmondson Avery Egerton-Warburton Brooke Egerton-Warburton Isabella Geraci Olivia Geraci	Morgan Gilfond Mariah Hesser Jasmine Hill Ava Humphrey Olivia Jarrett Grace Kennedy Rachel Lebda Charlotte Leone Ariane Lindsay Peyton Manna Erin McCarthy Charlotte McEvoy Kate Morton Louisa O'Reilly-Hyland Leandre Pestcoe Annelise Pizzitola Mia Rahn Carolina Ramirez	Margaret Rand Cloe Rankin Margaret Rashid Sara Rex Kathleen Ritchie Alice Roosevelt Charlotte Sanford Samantha Scales Bianca Scotto Elizabeth Shah Grace Sheppard Annika Solomone Isabel Sondey Alessia Spelman Schuyler Stump Maya Thompson Phoebe Tomlinson Delia Tyree

Class 1
Class of 2018

Elizabeth Acevedo
Emma Bellet
Gwen Bischoff
Reagan Brown
Nora Burke
Elizabeth Burns
Claire Burwell
Skylar Carroll
Sophia Centola
Rebecca Chen
Christine Coleman
Catherine Curry
Skylar Davis
Julia Faucetta
Ellen Gaffney
Margaret-Anne Guerin
Catherine Harrison
Georgiana Harrison

Isabella Hartman
Charlize Hebert
Olivia Heskett
Lana Hill
Lucia Holzheu
Georgia Husson
Charlotte Kelman
Sophia Klebnikov
Sofia Laffont
Julia Larson
Chloe Lazard
Eugenie Le Picart
Sophie Mackin
Sophia Mazzella
Lauren McCarthy
Katherine McEvoy
Carolyn Messina
Olivia Monahan

Nina Norton
Maria Sofia Pena
Katherine Pepi
Grace Perkins
Cathryn Rencricca
Alicia Rivera
Juliana Ruggieri
Catherine Rutherfurd
Ashley Scott
Alessia Seroff
Genevieve Jayne Sippel
Julia Spiegel
Olivia Truesdell
Grace Villano
Grace Wilson
Lily Wood

Class 2
Class of 2017

Whittier Ambrose
Nikki Bregman
Christina Brumbaugh
India Burns
Paris Calcagnini
Haley Campbell
Katherine Coleman
Lily Dillon
Jacqueline Dunne
Madeline Fouts
Laura Gallagher
Mattison Gibson
Anne Healy
Charlotte Healy
Anjali Iyer
Francesca Kehoe
Ryan Kilgallon

Christina Lorenc
Carolina Mahedy
Alessandra Marinaro
Daisy Miller
Katherine Mitchell
Cameron Munn
Samantha Munson
Caitlin Murphy
Morgan Murphy
Ariana Nakhla
Samantha O'Donoghue
Emma Paquette
Katharina Petermann
Alessandra Pichler
Alexandra Pisacane
Caroline Reinstadtler
Darcy Riano

Olivia Robbins
Winston Rossetter
Logan Rubin
Josefina Ruggieri
Annick Saralegui
Gabriella Scotto
Jennifer Shah
Grace Sheridan
Camille Shimshak
Davis Silver
Theodora Simons
Morgan Stephens
Arissa Tagatac Aoki
Ava Towey
Victoria Wahba
Hannah Waldron

Class 3
Class of 2016

Kiana Arcari
Nina Arcos
Stella Aykroyd
Katherine Beshar
Olivia Bousquette
Constance Caiola
Katherine Chamberlain
Chloe Coleman
Laura Conner
Avery Cross
Clare Curry
Grace Daly
Larissa Danovitch
Caitlin Ervine
Rose Farah
Janae Farmer
Cecily Graham

Helena Gray
Carina Hahn
Evan Haller-Hiser
Linda Hanson
Victoria Horrocks
Jessica Husson
Camila Johanek
Caroline Judelson
Suzanna Keough
Katrina Khan
Anna Kramer
Charlotte Lindsay
Beatrice March
Maggie McMahon
Annie McVeigh
Lauren Monahan
Samantha Mueller

Elizabeth Peck
Kira Petukhova
Alexandra Piegza
Lily Rahn
Sabrina Re
Julia Robinson
Laura Ruperez
Alexandra Sanford
Greta Schatz
Kelsey Schiltkamp
Charlotte Sippel
Aria Sundaram
Jacqueline Urwin
Alexandra Waldman
Elizabeth Wyckoff
Alexa Xylas

Class 4
Class of 2015

Camila Arria-Maury
Manuela Arria-Maury
Claire Bischoff
Charly Anne Bisso
Sophie Broadbent
Manzi Burns
Megan Clyne
Elena Conde
Emily Corrigan
Victoria Cox
Gillian Coyne
Pia De Giorgis
Mara Donadio
Gabrielle Doran
Olivia Doran
Morgan Dougherty
Jayda Farmer
Elizabeth Feeney

Isabella Gaspar
Caroline Glidden
Sophia Haggar Planchard
Ashley Keno
Megan Lasersohn
Elizabeth Lasusa
Helena Le Picart
Isabel Lindsay
Josephine Lupa
Sonia Main
Elena Malashenko
Reagan Menz
Jacqueline Messina
Renata Miller
Zharia Mohammed
Maria Angeles Molina
Devon Murphy
Victoire Neve

Carlin O'Neill
Valentina Onetti
Willow Pagan
Anastasia Pena
Geena Pullo
Hannah Riggins
Eloise Robert
Kelsey Robins
Kaleigh Scales
Emily Shah
Regina Soriano
Isabel Taylor
Keiko Turecamo
Victoria Villalba
Natalie Wall
Lily Young

CHAPTER 1

Mimi

A little mouse was hidden beneath a plant in the front hall. Workmen came and went and she watched it all. It was August and it was hot.

The mouse was Mimi and she lived with her mother, father, and little sister, Rosie, in a school called the Convent of the Sacred Heart in New York City. Mimi and Rosie had just come back from another Sacred Heart school in Greenwich, Connecticut. They had spent their summer in the country with Granny Annie. Granny Annie had accompanied them into the city so she could go to a special party.

"Why is there going to be a party?" Rosie had asked as they had traveled back to New York on a delivery truck.

"We are celebrating a very important anniversary," Granny Annie explained. "The school was started a hundred and twenty-five years ago."

"Was this the first Sacred Heart school?" Mimi asked.

"Heavens, no," said Granny Annie. "The very first Sacred Heart school was started in France more than two hundred years ago by a young woman named Madeleine Sophie Barat."

"Why?" Rosie wanted to know. "Why did she start the school?"

"Madeleine Sophie wanted to start a school for girls. In those days, most girls didn't go to school. She wanted the girls to know and love God. She wanted them to learn all kinds of things and love learning."

"Ah," Mimi sighed. She loved learning.

"Madeleine Sophie also taught the girls to help others and live together as a loving family," continued Granny Annie. "She especially wanted the girls to learn how to make smart choices."

Early this morning, Father Mouse had brought Mimi down to the front hall to hide in the planter near the main staircase. From her hiding spot, she could hear all kinds of conversations. It was important that the Mouse family know what was going on, especially now with dozens of workmen running about painting, poking holes in walls, and fixing things.

The school was housed in two elegant mansions on 91st Street, right across from Central Park. Upper and Middle School girls studied in the mansion on Fifth Avenue. Mimi and her family lived in the second building, where the younger girls had their classes.

The Mouse home was safely hidden behind a bookcase in a fourth grade classroom on the fifth floor. It was a lovely place, with little glass windows looking out onto a tiled terrace. There was plenty of food, too. Right down the hall was a snack table with cheese, crackers, and all kinds of treats.

Mimi thought a school was a wonderful place to live. Every day she could run up and down the little stairs in the walls and visit classes. When she wanted to practice her multiplication tables she went to the third grade. When she wanted to paint pretty pictures she spent the day in the kindergarten.

Mimi learned all kinds of things in this way. She learned how the Iroquois made longhouses and grew corn by watching fourth grade girls make a miniature Iroquois village. She peeked into the second grade classrooms when she wanted to improve her spelling or find out about New York City neighborhoods. Each spring, Mimi visited the first grade to watch the eggs crack open to reveal baby chicks. She especially loved to watch scientific experiments in the basement science lab. Mimi was never bored.

Last year, Mimi had made a friend—a girl friend. Her name was Maddie. Maddie was nine years old, just like Mimi. The two of them talked and shared secrets. Mimi helped Maddie study, and Maddie always kept her safely hidden from the other children.

"What fun it was," Mimi daydreamed, "when we . . ."

The little mouse looked down with a start. Two pairs of hungry eyes were looking up at her. The school's cats were on the prowl. The black one with white paws was named Pen. The other cat was a fluffy gray and he was called Pencil.

Mimi looked around. From the planter near the staircase, she could see the office of the Head of School. She jumped down and ran as fast as she could to find her friend, Midnight, who slept all day under Head of School's desk.

Midnight was a large, lovable dog. The black Labrador retriever had been found a few years ago tied to a street sign outside the school. Now he lived in the school and went home every night with the Head of School. All the children loved Midnight. After school they would stop by the office to see if Midnight wanted to take a walk around the block. Mimi loved her humble dog friend, too.

Mimi tore past Midnight with the cats right behind her. She jumped up on a chair and onto the desk and slipped into an empty coffee cup. While Mimi shivered with fright, Midnight joined in the chase.

"He must think we're playing a game," Mimi thought.

"Midnight, Pen, Pencil," someone called from the hall. "It's time to eat."

The three animals happily followed the voice out of the room.

"What a relief," Mimi said as she climbed out of the coffee cup. The little mouse hurried back to the front hall to wait for her father to pick her up and bring her home.

CHAPTER 2

Mimi Finds Some Cheese

Mimi was usually a cheerful mouse, but today she was sad. She missed her friend Maddie, who was starting Middle School. Mimi wouldn't see her anymore because Father Mouse wouldn't let Mimi visit the other building. Sacred Heart could be a very dangerous place for a mouse. The two cats, Pen and Pencil, were always roaming around looking for a mouse snack.

Mimi really wanted a new Sacred Heart friend but her father was making her stay within the walls today. It was the first day of school, and the building was much too busy for a mouse to be about.

The girls were very excited to be back at school for a new year. Mimi could hear laughing and playing coming from the driveway. She peeked out of the mouse hole. Suddenly, she saw a flash and heard someone say "Cheese."

"Yum, cheese," thought Mimi as she crept further out of her hole.

Mimi didn't know it, but the flash came from a camera. Two happy girls in gray jumpers and red and white checked pinafores were having their picture taken by their mother

for the first day of school.

"Say 'cheese', Fiona. You, too, Emma," said the girls' mother.

Mimi just couldn't help it. She tiptoed quietly out of her hole to find the cheese. Granny Annie chased after Mimi, "You know your father doesn't want you out here."

"But someone said 'cheese'," Mimi said. "Where is the cheese?"

Meanwhile, Pen and Pencil were in a dark corner in the driveway, looking at Mimi and Granny Annie. Their tongues hung out of their mouths. They wanted mice for breakfast.

Pen and Pencil dashed out of their corner and pounced toward Mimi and Granny Annie. The mice ran to the trash can to hide.

"Ahhh!" yelled Mimi and Granny Annie. Then they noticed a small hole in the trash can and climbed inside.

"Phew, we're safe now," Mimi said.

But Pen and Pencil were close behind. They jumped up to the wide rim of the trash can. Granny Annie and Mimi tumbled out of the hole onto the driveway. Granny Annie's glasses fell off, but Mimi picked them up and together they ran quickly into the mouse hole.

The cats jumped down from the trash can and headed toward the open door to the street. Fiona and her sister were standing in line waiting to shake hands with the Head of the Lower School, Mrs. Hult.

"Are those cats trying to leave Sacred Heart?" Mimi heard Fiona say to her little sister.

Fiona left Emma standing on line and went to pick up the cats.

"I like you," she told them, "but please don't try to leave the school." Fiona took the cats to the front of the line.

Mrs. Hult smiled, "Why, thank you, Fiona. We won't let Pen and Pencil wander into the driveway again."

In the mouse hole, Mimi gave Granny Annie her glasses.

"That was a close call," said Granny Annie.

Fiona had saved Mimi and Granny Annie, but Pen and Pencil were still prowling around the school with hungry grins.

CHAPTER 3

Mimi Looks for Cookies

One morning in October, Mother Mouse was baking heart cookies for Mater's Feast. It was a special day for the children of Sacred Heart.

"Why is it special?" asked Rosie, Mimi's little sister.

Mimi and Rosie were at the table in the mouse kitchen drinking their morning milk.

"Today Sacred Heart children all around the world celebrate their love for Mary," said their mother.

"Mary who?" asked Rosie.

"Mary, the mother of Jesus," Mimi told her sister.

"They call her 'Mater Admirabilis'—'Mother Most Admirable'," said Mother Mouse.

"What does she look like?" Rosie asked again.

"There is a wonderful painting of her beside the chapel in the other building," Mother Mouse continued. "Perhaps, one day, we'll take you there to see it."

"Why are you making heart-shaped cookies?" Rosie never seemed to run out of questions.

"We make them because Mater has a heart that is so loving," Mother Mouse explained to her little daughter.

A heavenly aroma filled the air as Mother Mouse turned from the oven with a tray of freshly baked cookies. Mimi reached for one.

"No, Mimi. These are for after lunch," her mother scolded.

"Please, Mother. May I have just one?"

Her mother was firm. "No, I told you, after lunch. You are just going to have to be patient."

But Mimi was not patient. She was determined to get her hands on a cookie.

"Now, Mimi, be a dear," said Mother Mouse, "and fetch some sugar for the frosting."

Mimi was allowed to go to the Lower School kitchen on the third floor of her building. She picked up a basket and hurried down the tiny stairs in the wall.

Suddenly she smelled something sweet. From the mouse hole under a large steel sink, she could see the whole kitchen. No one was there. She followed the scent with her nose—she had an excellent sense of smell for a tiny mouse—right up to the front of a big cart. A bright pink cloth was draped over the cart, and she wanted to see what was on top. Mimi clutched the soft fabric and little by little pulled herself up.

"Cookies!" she said with delight.

They were golden brown with pink frosting on top and shaped like a heart. Best of all, they were as big as Mimi and her mouth began to water. Mimi tried to lift a cookie but it was too heavy. She pulled and pulled and tumbled back when a piece broke off.

Footsteps in the hall outside the kitchen startled her, and she quickly put the piece of cookie in her apron pocket and slipped down under the pink cloth to the shelf below. The cart began to move.

After a very long while, it stopped. Mimi peeked out. She looked in wonder at a beautiful painted garden. Tall trees with glistening berries covered the walls. Colorful birds—blue and red—were flying around the trees. The painted garden started going up.

"Is this garden an elevator?" Mimi wondered.

Suddenly, the gate of the garden room opened and the cart moved forward again.

When at last it stopped, Mimi quickly jumped off and there before her was the most beautiful painting she had ever seen. In it a young woman in a rose-colored gown with golden stars around her head was sitting in a chair by a window. She had a sweet and gentle face and long, slender hands crossed over her lap. Beside the young woman was a white lily and at her feet was an open book.

"This must be Mater!" Mimi exclaimed.

Mimi was so entranced by the painting that she didn't notice a gray shape moving slowly toward her. She looked around. There was Pencil crouched low. Quicker than a blink of an eye, she squeezed behind the painting. Her heart was racing. She was trapped. Behind the cat's gray twitching tail, she could see a mouse hole in the pillar at the top of the stairs. Mimi didn't know what to do. Afraid, Mimi looked down and saw Pencil's sharp claws reaching for her.

Then the large wooden doors next to the painting opened and she heard, "The Mass has ended. Go in peace to love and serve the Lord."

A crowd of excited girls came out of the chapel. With them was Fiona. Laughing and talking with her friends, Fiona walked toward the cookie cart. When she saw Pencil, she turned and picked him up. She scratched the cat's ears and smoothed down the fur on his back. Mimi saw her chance and scurried along the wall until she came to the hole by the stairway.

The little mouse ran all the way home without stopping. She dashed into the mouse hole kitchen, exhausted and relieved to be safe. Looking at her mother's cookies, she suddenly felt sick. She reached into her apron pocket and threw away the piece of cookie she had found on the cart. Mimi had risked so much just because she couldn't be patient. She hugged her mother.

"Why, what is wrong, dear?" said Mother Mouse.

"Nothing," Mimi murmured. "I just love you, Mother."

CHAPTER 4

Mimi Hears a Story

Mimi greatly enjoyed her grandmother's visit. She felt very important when Granny Annie invited her to visit the Upper School Library. Mimi had never been there before and she was excited to have some special time alone with Granny Annie.

Granny Annie said it would be a quiet place where the two of them could talk, but she hadn't told Mimi it would be so grand. The ceiling of the library was very high and beautifully painted. There was a large fireplace and stone carvings on the wall. The most interesting part of the room, though, was the winding stone staircase that jutted out from the wall.

"What is that little staircase for, Granny Annie?" Mimi asked.

Granny Annie explained that once long ago this building belonged to a family named the Kahns.

"This room was Mr. Kahn's reception room. His bedroom was right above and the stairway curved around up to a door at the top. When people came to visit, he would come down these stairs and peek through the small window to see who was there. If he didn't feel like meeting with them, he would just sneak back up the staircase before they saw him."

"How silly!" exclaimed Mimi. "Did Mr. Kahn have any children?"

"Yes, he did. He had a charming wife named Addie and four darling children: Maude, Margaret, Gilbert, and Roger. In fact, I used to be quite good friends with Maude back when I was a little mouse and lived here with my family."

"You lived here, Granny?"

"Yes, and Maude and I were friends quite like you and Maddie are friends."

Granny Annie went on to tell Mimi about some of the good times and bits of mischief that she and Maude used to get into together.

"We loved to play on the secret staircase and spy on Mr. Kahn and his visitors. He sometimes had very important people stop by, such as a famous playwright named Eugene O'Neill and the conductor Arturo Toscanini."

Granny Annie told Mimi how she and Maude would nibble on bits of cake from the tea trays and pretend they were joining in with all of the important adults in the reception room.

"Other times, I would slide down the long, curving banister of the staircase," Granny Annie smiled, "with Maude giggling and chasing right behind me. Sometimes, though, Gilbert and Roger would try to catch me. Boys can be such trouble, but Maude would always come to my rescue.

"Maude was a true friend," said Granny Annie.

"That sounds like Maddie. She has always been such a

good friend to me, and it's hard not seeing her. I really miss her," Mimi said.

"I know just how you feel, Mimi. Eventually Maude grew up and went away to school, and I was very lonely. But the wonderful thing about friendship is you can always make another friend."

"Really?" Mimi sighed.

"After Maude went away, her little sister, Margaret, became my friend and we had many happy days together. You, too, will find another good friend. I know you will."

Granny Annie gave Mimi a warm hug.

"Now, my dear, I need to find a bit of reading for my long journey back to Greenwich. Let's see, this book should be just the thing. Now what have I done with my reading glasses? I always seem to be losing them."

"Granny Annie . . ."

"Yes?"

"They're on your head," Mimi replied with a giggle.

"Ah! So they are, so they are," smiled Granny Annie. "That seems to be the last place I look."

CHAPTER 5

Mimi Makes a Friend

It was Halloween and Mimi was watching the third and fourth grade girls get ready to go to the ballroom for the annual Halloween Parade. Fiona was dressed as a black and white cat just like Pen.

"Where is your tail, Fiona?" asked a classmate.

"Oh no, it must be here somewhere."

Fiona asked her teacher if she could stay behind to look for it. She dashed around the classroom and was in such a hurry that she stepped on Mimi's tail.

"Ouch!" cried Mimi.

"Oh my goodness, Pencil. I'm sorry if I hurt you. I'm looking for the tail that goes with my costume," said Fiona.

"I'm not Pencil. I'm Mimi. Your tail is over by the window."

"Thank you so much," said Fiona as she attached the tail to the back of her costume. She looked at Mimi again.

"Aren't you the mouse I saw on the first day of school?"

"That's right. I remember you, too," said Mimi. "I saw you last week outside the chapel."

The little mouse and the girl looked at each other for
a moment. Then Fiona said, "I must go. I'm late for the
Halloween Parade. Why don't you come down and watch?"
"I'd love to," Mimi said.

Mimi slipped into a hole in the wall as Fiona hurried down the stairs. She reached the ballroom just as Fiona joined her classmates in line. The children began to recite their Halloween poem,

Halloween is coming!
The witch is on her broomstick.
Halloween is coming!
I want to be a pumpkin or a cat.
Halloween is coming!
Black cats creeping in the night.
Halloween is coming!
Jack-o-lanterns everywhere.
Halloween is coming!
There are spirits in the air.
Halloween is coming!
Ghosts climbing up the ballroom stairs.
Halloween is coming!
School is full of spiders, bats, and black cat masks.
Halloween is coming!
Children singing scary songs.
Halloween is coming!
Oh, my goodness! BOO! It's HERE!

After the poem, the girls began parading down the center of the ballroom. One by one they showed their costumes to the Head of School and teachers. As Fiona walked toward the door, she noticed Mimi peering out of a hole by the baseboard. Quickly, she knelt down by the hole and pretended to tie her shoelace.

"Would you come back to our classroom for cupcakes and punch?" Fiona whispered.

Mimi gave a quick nod.

In a few minutes, Mimi arrived breathless at the mouse hole near the back of Fiona's classroom. Fiona saw her and set a napkin with a piece of cupcake down in front of the hole. She had included plenty of black and orange sprinkles.

"Thank you," Mimi said. "I'll give some to my little sister and parents."

All of a sudden, she remembered Granny Annie's advice and shyly asked, "Would you like to be my friend?"

"Of course I would." Fiona replied. "You live at Sacred Heart, so that means you are part of my Sacred Heart family. Will you come back and visit soon? I'd love to meet your family."

"Really? That makes me so happy," Mimi said. "I used to be friends with a girl named Maddie. She went to Middle School this year and my father won't let me go over there."

"Oh," said Fiona.

"Well, I have to go," Mimi said. "Enjoy the rest of the Halloween party. And be careful not to step on any more tails."

Fiona giggled and Mimi said goodbye, happy to have found a friend.

CHAPTER 6

Mimi Has an Adventure

Three weeks later, the Mouse family was busy getting ready for the Feast of Saint Philippine Duchesne. Mimi asked her parents if she could go hear the children sing.

"I'm sorry, Mimi," said Father Mouse, "but it's not safe for you. The music room is in the other building. Besides, we need your help with decorating for our dinner in honor of Philippine Duchesne."

Mother Mouse was making cornbread while Father Mouse cooked a wonderful stew. Rosie was at the table making decorations. Mimi watched.

"You know, Rosie, you are named for Philippine Duchesne," said Mother Mouse. "Her real name was Rose Philippine Duchesne."

"Who was she?" asked Rosie.

"She was a very brave woman who came to this country almost two hundred years ago. She was a pioneer who started the first Sacred Heart school not far from the Mississippi River. Life was often difficult for her but, because of her courage and hard work, there now are Sacred Heart schools all around the country."

Father Mouse added, "Philippine came from France and all her life she wanted to live with Native Americans. Many years later, when she was a very old woman, she went to live with some Native American people called the Potawatomi."

Mimi loved this story. She wondered if she could ever be as brave as Philippine Duchesne. Her family went back to cooking and Mimi could hear the distant voices of the girls singing in the music room. How she wanted to go and listen to the beautiful music.

"I will be brave," said Mimi.

When no one was looking, she slipped out and headed for the music room.

The passageways in the walls of the other building were dark, and the floors were cold and slippery. From the fifth floor mouse hole, she looked down a long empty hallway.

"Where is the music room?" she wondered. The singing had stopped.

Mimi ran down to a door at the end of the hallway. It was cracked open, so she ventured out. The air was crisp and chilly. No one was outside.

Mimi scampered over the rubber padding of a rooftop playground. Through the wire fence, she could see Central Park and—way off in the distance—the New York City skyline. It was November and there were still red, yellow, and orange leaves on the trees. She could see an enormous lake and people running on the path around it. It was so beautiful!

Mimi shivered. She wished she had brought her coat. She decided to go back in and look for the music room when

suddenly the door opened and out ran dozens of happy, screaming girls.

Mimi was surrounded by blue shoes running everywhere. She hoped she wasn't noticed. She kept trying to get to the edge of the playground but every time she went in one direction, she almost was stepped on. Some girls were playing jump rope, and Mimi hopped onto one of the shoes and grabbed onto the end of a shoelace.

Then it was the girl's turn to jump and Mimi was tossed up and down again and again. Before long, she lost hold of the shoelace and flew up into the air. Much to her surprise she landed softly in a pinafore pocket.

A hand reached in and touched her furry back.

"Mimi, is that you?" asked Fiona, surprised and happy. She quickly stepped to the side of the playground where her classmates couldn't see Mimi.

"Yes," replied the little mouse peering out of Fiona's pinafore pocket.

"Are you all right?"

"No."

"What's the matter?" asked Fiona.

"I went exploring," said Mimi, "and came out here. All of a sudden I was surrounded by blue shoes running everywhere. I almost was stomped on. Then I went flying in the air and here I am . . . in your pocket."

"It can get a bit wild out here," Fiona agreed. "We always run around and play with the jump ropes. If you want, we could play a different game."

"Not if there's any moving about in it," said Mimi as a Hula Hoop rolled by.

"We could play I spy," said Fiona. "You go first."

"I spy," said Mimi, "with my little eye, something starting with . . . *p*."

Fiona looked around. There at the other end of the playground were Pen and Pencil, stalking some unsuspecting sparrows.

"Pencil," said Fiona.

"No."

"Pen."

"No."

Fiona tried again, "Poppies."

"Fiona!" said Mimi. "It's autumn. The only red things are the red leaves still on the trees."

"I give up."

"I'll give you a clue," said Mimi, pointing to the park. "Look there."

Fiona turned around. "All I see is Central Park."

"That's it, park, Central Park," said Mimi.

"But Central Park starts with a *c*, not a *p*," said Fiona, laughing.

Twenty minutes later, Fiona delivered Mimi safely back to the Lower School building. Mimi worried that her parents were looking for her.

She slipped into the mouse kitchen, unnoticed. Phew!

CHAPTER 7

Mimi Makes Friends of an Unexpected Kind

Fiona and her class were having a special celebration in the classroom on the fifth floor. It was the Friday before Thanksgiving and the girls were eating pumpkin bread, apple pie, and turkey sandwiches, and drinking apple cider.

Mimi watched from a vent in the corner.

After a while, the teacher called the girls together.

"We have so much to be grateful for," she said. "There are people in our city who don't have all the things we have. So, let's plan a dinner for a family who wouldn't have Thanksgiving without our help. Every girl will bring some food for the meal and three dollars to buy a turkey," said the teacher.

"I'll bring the sweet potatoes."

"I'll get some beans."

"What about bread? I'll get that."

The girls were excited and all started to talk at once. Mimi wanted to help, too.

She remembered there were large plates of little cheese cubes in the Lower School kitchen.

"How will I get the cheese without people in the kitchen

seeing me?" she worried as she went down the tower stairs. On the fourth floor, she froze at the thunderous pounding of feet on the steps. The second grade was coming down from the roof playground.

"Oh no, more blue shoes—again!" She stayed very still at the edge of the step. She didn't know what to do. Should she go up or down?

Soon it was quiet again. Mimi ran as fast as she could down the tower stairs but went too far down. She didn't know where she was and ran out to the rotunda stairs to get her bearings. Then she saw Pen and Pencil.

The cats' eyes narrowed when they saw Mimi. The little mouse quickly climbed up to the red velvet railing and headed down. The cats followed her on the marble steps, faster and faster. They would get her at the end of the railing. But at the bottom, the marble floor was so slippery that the two cats slid right across the floor and hit the wall.

Bumped and bruised, they sat up, stunned.

Mimi peered down.

"I'm sorry. I didn't mean to make you hurt yourselves."

Suddenly, Mimi felt sorry for the poor cats. She had learned she should be thankful for everything and everyone, even her enemies.

There were bandages in the classroom, Mimi remembered. She found the bandages and ran back to the cats.

"Thank you, Mimi, for helping us," said Pencil softly, rubbing his sore nose with a paw. Pen was carefully licking a leg.

"How can we help you now?" they said with joy.

Mimi told them about the Thanksgiving boxes and how she wanted to give something, too.

Mimi and her new friends worked very hard during the next three days. Pen found a shoebox. Pencil found bits and scraps of colored paper and Mimi decorated the box. They all searched for leftover food to put in the box.

On Tuesday morning, their little shoebox was sitting in the rotunda beside all the other boxes, one from every class in the Lower School. Each box was decorated with colorful paper turkeys and red and yellow leaves. On the sides were heart-shaped signs which read "We love you."

The Head of School and Midnight had come to the rotunda to see the boxes. The dog was sniffing around and wagging his tail.

Mimi was excited. She climbed to the rim of one big box to see what was inside. Suddenly, she lost her footing and tumbled in headfirst. She landed on a bag of rice. All around her were cardboard walls and huge cans of beans and corn.

"Help!" Mimi cried.

Then she heard the door open and a man came to take the boxes to a delivery truck.

Midnight started barking.

"Don't worry, Mimi," purred Pen and Pencil, "we're here." While everyone was looking at Midnight and wondering why he was barking, Pencil reached a paw into the box. Mimi caught hold of it and climbed out.

Mimi rode back to her mouse home on Pen's back. She was happy.

The Thanksgiving boxes had
gone to families all over New York
City. She had helped those in need
and had made some new friends.

CHAPTER 8

Mimi Sees a Show

The Christmas season arrived at last. For Mimi, this was the best part of the year. Her birthday was right before Christmas, and the whole world seemed to be celebrating with her.

The children and the teachers were busy rehearsing for the Christmas shows. There were wreaths on every door and, in the rotunda by the marble staircase, there was a beautiful tree with twinkling lights and satin bows.

As soon as she woke up every day, Mimi hurried to the ballroom to watch the children say their morning prayers. She loved to hear the songs and see the candles lit on the Advent wreath.

One morning, Fiona lingered in the hallway when her class went back upstairs. Mimi ran out to meet her.

"Emma's class is doing a Christmas show on Wednesday and I'm going to be there. We could sit together. Will you come?" Fiona asked.

"I want to but you know I can't, Fiona. My parents won't let me leave this building," Mimi said sadly.

"Please come, Mimi. It's going to be a fabulous show."

"How could I ever get to the theater?" asked Mimi. "It's in the other building."

"Try, Mimi. There must be a way," said Fiona.

A little later, Mimi found Pen and Pencil in the banquet hall. They were sitting in a warm spot next to a heating vent. It was snowing outside and both cats were watching the large, wet snowflakes whirl past the tall window.

"Would you help me again?" Mimi asked them. "Fiona's little sister has a Christmas show on Wednesday, but I'm not allowed to go to the theater. Can you think of a way to get me there safely?"

"Hide in Midnight's fur," answered Pen and Pencil, still watching the snowflakes, tails sweeping back and forth behind them.

"Your mother and father won't be home that morning," said Pencil, turning toward her. "We heard them talking."

"They are going out to celebrate their 20th anniversary," added Pen. "They didn't say where."

"We'll tell Midnight to pick you up," said Pencil.

"And we'll meet you there," said Pen.

Mimi ran home and marked the day of the show on her calendar. All week, she danced and skipped and made up a poem.

Christmas Poem
Star light, star bright,
Beautiful star on Christmas night.

Christmas is Baby Jesus,
kind and nice as my sister Rosie.
Baby Jesus.
Star light, star bright,
Beautiful star on Christmas night.

Christmas is an angel,
beautiful, watching over me, as my granny.
Angel.
Star light, star bright,
Beautiful star on Christmas night.

Christmas is a star,
sparkly and shiny as Mater's crown.
Star.
Star light, star bright,
Beautiful star on Christmas night.

Christmas is Mary,
loving and beautiful as my mother.
Mary.
Star light, star bright,
Beautiful star on Christmas night.

Christmas is Joseph,
kind and good as Santa.
Joseph.
Star light, star bright,
Beautiful star on Christmas night.

Christmas is a Christmas tree,
sparkling and pretty as my birthday cake.
Christmas tree.
Star light, star bright,
Beautiful star on Christmas night.

Christmas is a candle,
friendly and glowing as the night stars.
Candle.
Star light, star bright,
Beautiful star on Christmas night.

Christmas is a reindeer,
big and strong and swift as my father.
Reindeer.
Star light, star bright,
Beautiful star on Christmas night.

Finally the day of the show arrived. At nine o'clock in the morning, Midnight ambled into the theater with Mimi safely hidden in his fur.

The room was filled with mothers, fathers, babies, and little brothers crawling under chairs. Sisters in gray jumpers and checked pinafores were on the floor in front. Fiona was sitting with them.

Midnight quietly trotted around the edge of the room and sat under the piano. Pen and Pencil were there already. Mimi peeked out, and when Fiona saw her friend, she moved closer to the piano. The lights dimmed and the show began.

Fiona was right. The show was fabulous. The second grade girls told the story of the birth of a baby in Bethlehem. Emma recited her lines perfectly. Some girls sang carols and others danced. It was beautiful.

Then the lights came up and it was over. Mimi sighed happily and looked up. There above her was the most beautiful chandelier she had ever seen. Hundreds of little glass pieces sparkled from twelve candle lights all around it. It was more beautiful than her birthday cake.

"Oh," murmured Mimi, her eyes fixed on the dazzling light.

Suddenly, Midnight stood up. Mimi wasn't holding on and tumbled to the floor.

"Mimi, what are you doing here?" said Mimi's mother and father.

They were sitting in the arched grooves of the golden frame of a mirror hanging next to the piano. Two little panels in the frame were missing, and the two mice had comfortable seats and a fine view of the Christmas show.

Mimi didn't know what to say.

Mother Mouse looked at Mimi's father.

"It is Mimi's birthday today," she said.

Father Mouse dashed out of a small hole below the mirror and brought Mimi safely in as people began to leave the theater.

Mother Mouse hugged her little mouse.

"Happy Birthday, Mimi, dear," she said.

"You know, Mimi," said Father Mouse. "Christmas really is

all about love. That's what we learned from the show. We do love you and so we're happy you got to come today."

The three mice set off for home, arm in arm.

CHAPTER 9

Mimi Gets a Big Surprise

One morning in early February, Mimi was playing with her yo-yo when suddenly a huge piece of paper slid under her door. It was a letter from Fiona.

"Please come with me to an ice-skating party in Central Park. All the girls at Sacred Heart are invited. It will be a big Valentine's Day party," it said. "Meet me in the rotunda at six o'clock on Monday night. Love, Fiona."

Mimi jumped up and down and twirled around. Then she remembered she would have to ask her father.

Mimi found him reading his newspaper in the mouse kitchen and showed him the letter. He shook his head.

"Absolutely not."

Mimi begged and begged.

"Central Park is not a safe place for a little mouse," he said firmly.

Mimi ran to her room and slammed the door. She threw herself on her little bed and soaked her pillow with tears. After a long while, she calmed down and got up and went to her desk.

"Dear Fiona," she wrote on a tiny piece of paper. "My father won't let me go. I'm so sorry. Love, Mimi."

Mimi peered into Fiona's classroom. The children were not there. She found Fiona's locker and slipped the note through the crack at the bottom.

She ran home and went straight to bed. She was very tired and fell fast asleep.

Mimi heard the ringing of a distant bell.

"What is it?" At first she was frightened. The sound was coming from the courtyard.

The courtyard was in the other building, but Mimi knew about a secret passageway that led from the second floor of her building under the theater and out to the courtyard. It was under the floor and safe for a little mouse like Mimi. She ran quickly and came to a hole beside a beautiful fountain on the courtyard steps. Mimi looked out, amazed by what she saw.

The air was frosty and it was getting dark, but the courtyard was aglow with light and color. Ribbons and hearts—all red, Mimi's favorite color—were hanging everywhere. Candles on the wall ledges were lit and tiny pink lights blinked on and off from the balconies above. Fiona was standing in the middle, ringing a bell.

In the corner there was a shoebox table with tiny cheesecakes, decorated with hearts. The fountain on the steps was filled with her favorite drink and there were sweet cherries floating on top.

Best of all, in the middle of the courtyard was a small ice-skating rink. Mimi went closer to see. Beside it she saw a pair of tiny skates just her size.

"Beautiful . . ." said Mimi, breathless with wonder.

"I was so sad when you said you would miss the ice-skating party," Fiona said. "So I decided to bring the party to you."

"Oh, thank you, thank you, thank you, Fiona," Mimi said through happy tears.

"Why don't you put these on and try it," Fiona said, handing her the little ice skates.

Mimi and Fiona skated together for a long time. Mimi twirled and swirled and spun around and around the rink. As she went she made up a poem.

Love is giving,
Love is kind,
Will you be my Valentine?

Love is sharing, love is caring,
Love is giving, love is forgiving,
Love is playing, love is praying.
Love is living, love is giving.

Kind as a kitten purring,
Kind as a friend hugging,
Kind as a baby smiling,
Kind as a bunny sharing a carrot,
Kind as mouse sharing its cheese.

Love is giving,
Love is kind,
Will you be my Valentine?

"Mimi, dinner is ready," called Mother Mouse.

Mimi woke up and smiled. That afternoon, she knew she had found a good and dear friend in Fiona.

CHAPTER 10

Mimi's Lost and Found

It was a cold Saturday in March. Mimi and Rosie were playing hide-and-go-seek in the rotunda. Mimi covered her eyes and counted while Rosie hid.

" . . . ninety-eight, ninety-nine, one hundred." Mimi opened her eyes. She dashed to the bookcase and peeked behind. Rosie wasn't there. She ran to the book basket. She wasn't there either. Mimi looked everywhere. Her little sister was gone. Mimi ran home as fast as she could go.

"Mother, Father," she cried, out of breath. "I've lost Rosie! We were playing hide-and-go-seek. I've searched and searched and I can't find her."

Her mother and father looked at each other.

"I said 'olly, olly oxen free' a thousand times." Mimi started to cry.

"Stay here with your mother," Father Mouse said. "I'll go search the building."

Mother Mouse had Mimi sit down with a cup of peppermint tea and a bit of blueberry muffin.

The Mouse family didn't know that Rosie had found a sweater on a bench in the rotunda. It had a nice snug pocket and Rosie crawled inside to hide.

The sweater belonged to the Head of the Lower School, Mrs. Hult. The morning before, Mrs. Hult had left the sweater on a bench while she talked with a teacher. Then she forgot all about it.

On Saturday, while Mimi counted and Rosie hid, Mrs. Hult had walked by the rotunda. When she saw her sweater, she picked it up with a terrified little mouse in the pocket.

Mrs. Hult was on her way to the chapel to make arrangements for the First Communion ceremony on Sunday. She put her sweater on a pew and, as soon as she walked away, Rosie scampered out. The little mouse ran to the corner of the pew and sat there shaking. Rosie didn't know where she was or what to do.

Meanwhile it was a long time before Father Mouse returned. Mimi and her mother were sitting in the kitchen when he came home the next morning.

"I've searched up and down in every room of the Lower School building," he said wearily. "She isn't here."

"That means she must be in the other building," Mother Mouse said.

"Please let me go with you," Mimi begged. "I really want to help."

"We'll all go," said Mother Mouse.

The three mice hurried through the secret passageway under the theater floor and came up into the wide hallway on the second floor. They heard the faint squeak of a little mouse.

"Rosie, where are you?" Father Mouse called.

"Here," cried Rosie. "I'm stuck in a vase." Her voice was small and far away.

The mice squeezed under the chapel door and found Rosie trapped in a huge vase at the far end of the room.

"How in the world did you get in there?" Mother Mouse asked.

"It was dark last night. I fell in . . ." Rosie said with a sob.

"Never mind," said Father Mouse. "Let's try to rock it over." The vase was heavy and wouldn't budge.

"I know," said Mimi. "Fiona will be here soon. Her little sister Emma's First Communion is today."

"Someone went to get flowers for the vase," Rosie wailed. "I heard them say so."

There was no time to lose. Mimi would have to go all alone to look for Fiona while Father Mouse kept watch at the chapel door and Mother stayed with Rosie.

Mimi hid in the large planter near the main staircase, where she had a view of the whole front hall. Parents and grandparents dressed for a special occasion were coming in, and little girls in white dresses were standing together in groups talking and giggling and jumping up and down.

"There she is!" Mimi watched as Fiona made her way through the crowd to the stairs.

As Fiona brushed past the planter, Mimi grabbed on to her coat sleeve and slipped into her pocket.

"What's wrong, Mimi?" Fiona knew right away that it was Mimi in her pocket. She moved quickly away from the crowd

and pulled Mimi out.

"Rosie's stuck in a vase in the chapel," said Mimi. "The ceremony is about to start."

"Don't worry," said Fiona.

She ran up the steps two at a time and into the chapel through the side door.

"Why, Fiona, what are you doing here?"

It was Mrs. Hult, holding a large bouquet of flowers.

"I . . . only wanted to see if the chapel looks different . . . from when I made my First Communion," stammered Fiona.

Mrs. Hult nodded and turned to unwrap the flowers.

Fiona quickly walked down the aisle and reached in the vase and scooped Rosie out. She put the little mouse gently in her other pocket. Fiona found the mouse parents by the back stairs and set Mimi and Rosie down beside them.

"Fiona dear, how can we ever thank you?" said Mother Mouse, hugging Rosie tightly.

Father Mouse shook his head. "Well, thanks to you, Rosie came to no harm."

"Would you like to come with me to see the First Communion ceremony?" asked Fiona.

There was room in the side pocket of Fiona's purse for the whole mouse family. Fiona found her mother and father and managed to get a seat on the aisle.

The music began. Mimi watched happily as the first little girl in a white dress walked slowly down the aisle. On her head was a crown of white flowers with a delicate white veil hanging down her back.

CHAPTER 11

Mimi Paints Some Eggs

Mimi was feeling blue. It was April and though the sun was bright, the wind outside was chilly. There were no pink blossoms on the cherry trees in Central Park. Their branches were empty and gray. A few daring daffodils had appeared out of the cold, muddy earth.

Life had been very dull for two long weeks. All the children had left the school in March for their spring vacation. The building was quiet. She hadn't heard Midnight's cheerful barking in days. There was no one at school to take care of a dog, so he went home with the Head of School.

She hadn't seen Pen and Pencil, either. The two cats were safely locked up in the laundry room with food and water.

"They're probably taking a long nap on the washing machine," Mimi thought glumly.

Her dear friend Fiona had left, too. And she had gone far, far away to Rome for her vacation. Mimi missed her every day.

"What's the matter, Mimi, dear?" said Mother Mouse one morning.

"I'm sick," said Mimi, holding her stomach. "I think I ate some bad cheese."

Mother Mouse turned away from her baking to look at Mimi.

"Are you sure it isn't that you miss Fiona?" she said kindly.

"I do miss her," Mimi said softly.

"I have an idea," Mother Mouse smiled. "Why don't you paint some eggs for our baskets? Tomorrow is Easter. We'll make a basket of eggs for Fiona, too. She'll be back on Tuesday, you know."

Mimi started to feel better. Three more days.

Father Mouse had brought home some plain wooden beads from a kindergarten classroom. They were just the right size for a little mouse's Easter basket.

Mimi and Rosie set to work.

"What is Fiona's favorite color?" asked Rosie.

"She doesn't have a favorite color," said Mimi. "She likes every color."

"Good! Let's make all the colors," said Rosie.

The sisters dipped Q-tips into the little round trays of watercolor paint. They painted some beads daffodil yellow, some sky blue, some morning-glory purple, and some rosy pink. They worked all afternoon.

Mimi then made little paper roses and put them in the cracks of the basket for Fiona. The roses were red—Mimi's favorite color. She tied her favorite red ribbon on the handle. The basket was beautiful.

Mimi sat down and wrote a note to put in the basket.

"Dear Fiona," it said. "I miss you. I am so glad you will be back soon. I hope you had a very happy Easter in Rome. Love, Mimi."

She ran to Fiona's desk and carefully put the little basket inside.

Mimi felt so much better and skipped all the way home.

CHAPTER 12

Mimi Says Goodbye

It was Prize Day, the last day of the school year. Mimi woke up with butterflies in her stomach. Today she would say goodbye to her dearest friend. This was Fiona's last day in the Lower School. Next year Fiona would go to Middle School in the other building, just like Maddie, and Mimi wouldn't see her anymore.

The Prize Day ceremony was in the ballroom, one of Mimi's favorite places. Her whole family was going to the ceremony. Even Granny Annie.

A week ago, the Lower School girls had returned from Field Day in Connecticut. Granny Annie had snuck into a girl's backpack. Everyone was so exhausted when they reached the city, no one noticed a mouse dashing off into the building.

When the Mouse family entered the ballroom, it was empty. They ran around the edge of the room to their places at the top of the fireplace. Mimi looked up and stopped.

"It's like a castle," Mimi thought, her eyes sparkling with delight.

The room had three tall doors made of mirrors on one side and marble columns on the other. The fireplace was at the far end of the room, with an oval mirror above it. At the other end there was a green and gold tapestry framed with red velvet. Above her, Mimi could see white cherubs made of plaster.

"We're here to protect you," they seemed to say. "Be strong and brave and always pray to God for help."

There were long rows of chairs on each side and a narrow pink carpet running down the middle. A lovely June breeze came through the open windows and the sun streamed in, casting golden light on the wooden floor.

Mimi heard footsteps outside. Quickly, she ran up a brocade window drapery and leaped into the grand piano in the corner of the room.

"Phew, safe!" Mimi breathed a sigh of relief as teachers started filling the seats under the tapestry.

A few moments later, someone sat on the piano bench and the processional music began. Mimi tried to avoid the piano hammers that were striking metal strings to make beautiful music. Mimi was tossed up and over like an acrobat as the music went faster and faster.

Then a long chord was played. Quickly, Mimi climbed out of the piano and ran as fast as she could along the windows behind the girls. Out of breath, she found her family sitting above the fireplace.

It took several minutes for Mimi to calm down enough to listen to the songs. Then each girl stood when her name was called and curtsied. Two by two, girls in beautiful dresses walked slowly down the center to receive their prizes and

promotion cards from Mrs. Hult and the Head of School. Tears in her eyes, Mimi watched Fiona receive her card.

"This is it," she said softly to herself. "It's time to say goodbye."

After the ceremony, Mimi ran upstairs to pack her suitcase. She and Rosie were leaving tomorrow to spend the summer with Granny Annie in Connecticut. As she closed her suitcase, her mother and father appeared at the door. They were smiling.

"Mimi, guess what?" Mother Mouse said.

Mimi looked up.

"We've made a decision," Father Mouse said. "You have studied hard this year. You've been kind and helpful in many ways. Most important, you have shown us that you know how to make smart choices. So we are going to let you go to the other building, starting in the fall."

"I'm so proud of you, Mimi," Granny Annie chimed in.

For once Mimi wasn't able to speak at all. Her heart was full of joy. She couldn't wait for a new school year to begin. She would be able to visit Fiona and Maddie. Maybe she would make some new friends, too.

"Thank you, Mother, thank you, Father," she managed to say and hugged them both.

She ran down to the front hall to find Fiona and share the good news.

Fiona was saying goodbye to her teachers and classmates. Mimi nibbled on her big toe.

"Fiona, I have great news," she said when Fiona picked her up. "My parents are allowing me to visit you in the

Middle School next year."

"Oh, Mimi! Think of all the adventures we'll have."

Mimi smiled.

"Happy?" asked Fiona.

"Yes," said Mimi. "I'm happier than I've ever been in my whole life."

The End